Moving On

Story by Dawn McMillan

Illustrations by Meredith Thomas

Contents

Chapter 1
Harsh Words

The maths class was over and school had finished for the day. Tess and her friend Laura gathered their books and rushed out to the corridor. Tess was excited. She and her brother, Nathan, were going to their dad's place for the weekend. They were going to cook dinner with Gran. "I love cooking!" Tess told Laura. "We're going to make spaghetti bolognaise."

In her hurry, Tess accidently bumped into someone in the corridor. "Watch it!" a voice snapped. Tess turned to see that she had knocked into Briar Davis, the new girl. Books and pens from Briar's bag had spilled all over the floor.

"Sorry!" Tess said, as she bent down to help Briar with her things. "I didn't see – "

"Forget it!" said Briar, crossly. "Just look where you're going next time, will you!"

Tess felt the colour rise in her face. Briar was being rude to her again, and she wondered why.

"Let's go, Tess," Laura said quietly. "Don't worry. She'll get over it." She walked with Tess towards the school gate. "Look! Your gran's here to meet you and Nathan."

Tess felt a little better when she saw Gran waiting at the gate.

When Tess arrived home at Dad's house, she waited for an opportunity to talk to Gran about Briar. As she chopped the onions for the bolognaise sauce, tears ran down her face.

"Ha! Onions make you cry," Nathan laughed and scooped his chopped tomatoes into a bowl. "See, I've finished the tomatoes already!"

"Then you can go and set the table, please, Nathan," said Gran.

Once Nathan had disappeared with a handful of knives and forks from the drawer, Gran put her arm around Tess. "It's not just the onions, is it, Tess?" she said. "What's wrong?"

Tess put the knife down. "It's school," she said. "It's this new girl called Briar. She's so rude to me, Gran!"

Gran turned the stove off. "Let's have a cup of hot chocolate," she said.

"So, what happened today, then?" Gran asked, handing Tess her drink.

"It's not just about today, Gran," Tess said, wiping the tears from her face. "It happens nearly every day!"

"Goodness!" Gran said, as she sipped her hot chocolate. "You say she's only been at school for a short time? Well, perhaps things will settle down. You never know what problems other people might have. Maybe there's something worrying her."

"But why is Briar only mean to me?" Tess asked, sniffing. "She's all right with the other girls!"

"Mmmm," Gran said, looking worried. "Well, I suppose all you can do is to give her time. Just be polite, but don't try to be her friend. Not yet."

"And it's not just Briar," Tess said quietly. "It's Dad, too."

"Your dad's been rude to you?" Gran was shocked.

"No! But he's different, Gran." Tess was crying again. "I can't explain. It's sort of like he's not thinking about us any more."

"Oh, dear," said Gran. "Your dad would be so upset to know you feel like this. I think he's just a bit distracted. Now that he and Mum have separated, he's finding new friends and thinking about what he wants to do with his life. But Tess, you must always remember that your dad loves you and Nathan so much. Even more than you love cooking!" Gran smiled as she went back to the stove.

Chapter 2
The Truth Is Out

After dinner, Gran had a quiet word to Dad while they cleaned the dishes. Then, Dad turned to Tess and Nathan and said, "Let's head down to the skatepark. Get your scooters and safety helmets from the shed."

A few moments later, Dad came out to find Tess and Nathan in the shed. "I'll get my old skateboard and my helmet, too. I haven't been on my board for years!" he laughed.

On the way to the skatepark, Nathan chatted excitedly about school. "I'm in a football team now, and I got top marks for my maths test!"

"That's fantastic, Nathan. Well done," Dad said. "Tess, how are you doing?"

Tess shrugged. "I'm okay," she said quietly.

"Well, I don't think you are," Dad answered, "and I think it's time I talked to you both. Let's sit under the tree over there."

They all sat down, and then Dad continued, "You see, things are changing for me. I have a new friend and I really like her. Her name is Evelyn Davis, and she's a teacher at the college. She has a daughter who goes to your school … in your class, Tess, I think."

Suddenly, Tess felt sick. Dad's new friend was Briar Davis's mother! Tess jumped up. "I'm not going to the skatepark!" she said crossly. Now she realised why Briar was so rude to her. Briar knew about Dad!

"So," Tess said sharply, "I suppose Ms Davis and Briar are going to live with you! It's our place too, Dad! Remember, we fixed up the gate, and did the painting, and …"

Nathan sat still and white-faced while Tess shouted at Dad.

"Just a minute, Tess," Dad interrupted, "let's talk about this properly. I have to be honest with you both. One day, Evelyn and I might want to live together, but not yet. We'll all work that out, if the time comes."

Tess stared at Dad.

"Tess," Dad said gently, "it will work out. I promise."

And Nathan added, "Please, Tess, come to the skatepark with us. I want to show you my trick on the ramp."

Chapter 3
The Science Project

At school, Tess avoided Briar, until the unthinkable happened. Ms Jamieson sorted the groups for the Science Fair projects. "Four to a group," she said, reading from her list of names. Tess held her breath. She was with Laura and Thomas. And then … Ms Jamieson called Briar's name.

Tess felt dizzy. *Briar!* She'd have to ask Ms Jamieson to change the group. And then Tess heard Ms Jamieson say that she wouldn't have people swapping groups.

Tess looked across at Briar. She saw the concern on her face. *Briar does know about Dad,* thought Tess. *She's probably worried about living with me!* And then Tess felt annoyed again. "Briar needn't think she's going to share my dad!" Tess muttered to Laura.

Laura looked mystified. "What do you mean?" she asked, but Tess just shook her head.

"We need a great topic," said Laura, when they sat down to their first Science Fair group meeting. "Any suggestions?"

"Insects!" said Tom, straight away. He was obsessed with spiders.

Tess hesitated. She didn't want to spend four weeks studying insects, but she was sure Briar would dismiss any suggestion she made.

"That's good," said Briar, sounding as doubtful as Tess felt. "But what about weather?"

"Weather is a great topic." Tess was surprised to hear the words come out of her mouth. "I could make illustrations of the water cycle."

Briar appeared to ignore Tess. "I'll research climate change," she said.

Laura was nodding and typing up tasks next to each of their names.

After four weeks of planning, researching, writing and illustrating, Tess took her mum to the Science Fair in the school hall.

"Wonderful, Tess!" Mum said, looking closely at the display Tess's group had completed. "You've all done such a great job! I love your water cycle diagrams, and the work on climate change is good, too."

"Briar found out a lot about climate change," Tess said.

"Briar Davis?" asked Mum, carefully.

"Do you know about Dad and Ms Davis, Mum?" Tess said quietly.

"Yes, I do, Tess, and I'm glad your dad has a new friend. Are you and Briar friends, too?" Mum asked.

"Not likely!" Tess answered quickly. "Briar doesn't like me, Mum. She was really rude to me at first. We managed to work together on the project, but we didn't talk much."

"Well, it sounds like things are improving. Maybe Briar's getting to know you better." Mum smiled, and they moved on to look at the other displays.

Chapter 4

Heading for the Coast

Tess knew they would have to meet Briar's mother sometime, but she was surprised when Dad suggested a shared trip to the coast.

"We can do some surfcasting," he said. "It'll be great fun."

"Yes!" Nathan shouted enthusiastically. "I love fishing!"

"So do I, but not with Ms Davis! Not with Briar!" Tess muttered under her breath.

"Come on, Tess," Dad said lightly, ruffling her hair, "let's see how it goes. We'll take two cars so we can come home when we want to."

To her surprise, Tess found that she liked Ms Davis – or Evelyn, as she asked Tess and Nathan to call her. She was quiet and friendly, and Tess noticed the way she stood back to let Dad and Nathan spend time fishing together.

But Briar was grumpy. "Nathan won't catch much with that small rod!" she said. Later, when Nathan did catch a fish, she wouldn't look at it.

Briar didn't want lunch, either. "No pie for me," she muttered.

"You need to eat something, Briar," Evelyn said calmly, and passed Briar a picnic plate. "You can have sandwiches and fruit if you don't want the pie."

The only time Tess saw Briar smile was when they all slid down the sand dune, to fall together at the bottom.

"Again!" Briar shouted.

"Yes!" laughed Tess, shaking sand from her clothes.

Chapter 5

Disaster!

Rolling down the dunes was hilarious, until Tess screamed with pain. "My arm!" she cried. "I hit that rock! I think it's …"

Nathan and Briar scrambled to their feet. Briar crouched down beside Tess. "Don't move," she said. "Here," she added, taking off her jumper, "this'll keep you warm. Nathan! Get your dad!"

While Nathan ran for help, Briar sat with Tess, talking quietly and telling her everything would be all right. Through her pain, Tess was surprised to realise that Briar really cared about her. "I thought you hated me," she whispered.

Briar shook her head. "Not really," she answered. "I just felt scared about sharing my mum and …"

But before Briar could say any more, Dad and Nathan and Evelyn were at Tess's side.

"Goodness," said Dad, with a worried expression. "I think that's broken, Tess. You're being so brave! Let's use my jumper as a sling, and we'll take you to the hospital."

"Come on," Dad said to Tess, "let's get you to the car."

Evelyn pulled her phone from her pocket. "Shall I call an ambulance, John?" she asked.

"No," Dad replied. "Thanks, Evelyn, but I don't think we need an ambulance. We'll be at the hospital in no time."

"We have some cushions in our car, and a blanket," Briar said, and raced away to get them.

"Right, there you are," said Dad gently, as he and Nathan made Tess as comfortable as they could in the back seat of the car. "Nathan, Evelyn can take you to Mum's house, if you don't want to come to the hospital."

But Nathan remained sitting beside Tess.

"I'll come with you, too," Briar said. "If you don't mind driving back alone, Mum?"

Evelyn smiled and shook her head. "You go with Tess, Briar. I'll drive you home from the hospital later."

Chapter 6
An Unexpected Gift

After Tess's arm had been plastered, her mum came to the hospital to take her home.

"There," said Mum, arranging Tess's pillows on the sofa, "how are you feeling now?"

"I'm okay," Tess answered, trying not to cry, "but I wish it hadn't happened!"

"You'll be fine in a few weeks, Tess," Mum said. "Luckily it wasn't a bad break."

"Hey, Tess," grinned Nathan, "I can stay home from school tomorrow to keep you company!"

"No skipping school, young man," Mum laughed. "You can keep Tess company when you get home."

Tess had plenty of company the next afternoon. Dad and Gran came to visit, their arms full of get-well presents.

"Thank you," Tess said, as Nathan helped her tear the paper from her parcels.

Then, Dad said, "There's one more, from Briar."

"Briar?" Tess whispered.

"Briar?" Mum grinned. "Well, I think I'll make Gran and Dad some coffee while you open that parcel."

In Briar's parcel, Tess found a set of three marker pens, and a note.

Hi Tess,
Hope you're okay. Here are some pens
so we can all write on your plaster.
Mum says, get well soon.
See you at school.
Your friend,
Briar

Tess read the note again. *Your friend, Briar.* Yes, now she knew that Dad was right. Everything was going to work out.